BUDAPEST/48

A RYAN LOCK STORY

SEAN BLACK

SBD

ABOUT THE BOOK

About The Story

It sounded too good to be true. Fly into Budapest. Handle the exchange in a straightforward kidnap for ransom case. Fly back home.

Total time involved: 48 hours.

But as private security operators Ryan Lock, and Ty Johnson are about to discover, there is no such thing as easy money.

AUTHOR'S NOTE

Budapest/48 is a standalone story of 19,000 words. To give regular readers a point of comparison, the full-length Lock novels average around 70,000 words.

As this is an exclusive international e-book edition it should be noted that spellings are American-English. British readers who feel short-changed by the lack of vowels may contact me via the website (seanblackbooks.com), and I will forward replacement vowels for them to insert into the text where required.

Have fun reading Budapest/48, but always remember, if you can see the whites of their eyes then you're too bloody close!

Sean Black
    March 15th, 2015

1

On the surface there was nothing extraordinary about Michael Lane's kidnapping. Apart from taking place in a part of the world not particularly known for cases of kidnap for ransom – that dubious honor goes to Latin America – it was pretty much a textbook case.

The thirty-four-year-old British national was snatched a little after six o'clock on a bitterly cold Monday morning in early December. The abduction took place as he was leaving his two-bedroom apartment on Hild Ter in Budapest's District 5 to go to work at his company's office on Tüzér Street in District 13.

According to the only known eyewitness, an elderly neighbor walking his dogs, a dark sedan had been parked at the curb along from the apartment entrance for ten minutes before Michael left for work. It was black, or dark blue, and of German manufacture. In this part of the city, which lay on the Pest side of the Danube, such cars were not uncommon

When Michael walked past, the rear passenger door opened. A slender, middle-aged white male in a dark-colored raincoat stepped out of the vehicle, blocking Michael's path. The kidnapper pointed what appeared to be a firearm at Michael and bundled him into the back of the car. The rear windows were heavily tinted. The car took off at speed towards the river.

Minutes later the sedan was lost in traffic. The vehicle surfaced two days later, burnt out on an abandoned lot in the Kőbánya area of District 10. Michael, a business analyst with a specialist knowledge of Central and Eastern European markets, who had only been posted by his American owned company to their new Budapest office a few months earlier, was gone.

Typically, the abduction part of a kidnap for ransom takes place in the morning, and close to the target's home or work. The reason for that is simple enough. To abduct someone, you first have to know where to find them. Taking someone from inside their home involves getting past some form of security — a doorman, or cameras, or even just a couple of locked doors. That's usually enough to rule it out. The street works better.

The most obvious pattern to establish in a person's life is their morning journey to work. After work they may go shopping, or to dinner, or to the theatre. Dinner may involve one route, the theatre quite another. They may leave early, or stay late.

The longer the kidnappers have to wait for their victim to be in position, the higher the chance they have of being spotted. From the kidnappers' perspective, the shorter that time is, the better. The same goes for the final stage: the exchange. If a kidnapper can reduce time on that end, they will.

As crimes go, kidnapping for ransom boils down to one single factor: time. That was why the time between abduction and the kidnappers contacting the victim's family or employer had a term all of its own. It was known as 'The Wait', thought it could have been as easily called the weight because every second of silence that ticked by without news of the victim offered its own excruciating agony to their loved ones.

Following this particular kidnapping there followed a series of phone calls between Budapest, Michael's wife in London, his company's head office in New York, and more calls to London, this time to the insurance broker who had organized the company's kidnap and ransom insurance policy. A negotiation team was called in. Talks began. Weeks later the ransom amount was finalized.

Now came the exchange. That required someone with specialist skills, and a very specific temperament. An individual or individuals who was accustomed to dealing with high pressure situations that involved safeguarding life.

A call was made to an unlisted cell phone number in Los Angeles.

2

L os Angeles International Airport

RYAN LOCK PULLED his Audi into a spot next to the elevator on the second floor of the parking structure. In the front passenger seat, Lock's business partner, Ty Johnson, shifted uncomfortably in his seat, ill at ease with something.

Lock shot him a look. "What?"

"Nothing," said Ty.

Lock put the car in park, and set the motion-activated camera he used when the car was going to be left for a prolonged period. If anyone entered the car, it would immediately relay the footage to him wherever he was in the world. The car was also fitted with a tracking device. Partly it was to do with the car's value – the basic model of the car cost north of a hundred thousand dollars, and that was before the customization that had been done on this particular vehicle. Lock had also acquired a lot of enemies over the years. He looked around the interior, making sure he was set. Ty was still glaring at him from behind his Oakley sunglasses.

"It's clearly not nothing," said Lock.

"You know this short-term parking is like thirty bucks a day. It costs like double what the lot around the corner does," said Ty.

Lock smiled to himself. Ty could be weird with money. He liked to flash it but he had a careful side borne out of an impoverished child-hood in Long Beach. "Client's covering all expenses. Airport parking included."

"Okay," huffed Ty. "As long as it ain't coming out of my share, know what I'm saying?"

TURNING LEFT into the Upper Class cabin on their scheduled Virgin Atlantic flight to London seemed to cheer Ty somewhat. The two men slid into their seats, ready for the ten hour flight.

Lock watched as Ty checked out the attractive young female crew members as they flitted back and forth, making sure that the passengers were settled and comfortable for the ten hour flight ahead.

"Tyrone?" said Lock.

Ty didn't look over. His eyes stayed fixed on a petite young blonde flight attendant who was busy serving drinks a few seats down. "Yup?"

"Eyes front, and roll your tongue back in," said Lock. "Business, remember?"

"Dude, she likes me," said Ty.

"Dude," said Lock, "you're sitting in a six thousand dollar seat. Of course she's going to pretend she likes you."

Ty finally looked over at Lock. "Pretend? Man, you're ruining this for me."

Lock opened a manila folder, and began to flick through the contents one more time. "Pop quiz," he said to Ty. "Who's the package?"

"Michael Lane. British national. Thirty-four-years-old. White. Mom was a journalist for The London Times, and his father worked in finance in the City of London. Married for seven years to Jan. She's back in London. One child, Grace. Two years of age. Mr.. Lane is believed to be in good health. Or at least he was at the time of abduction. No underlying medical conditions. Ran the London marathon two years ago."

Ty began to lever himself up from his seat. Lock reached over and pulled him back down. It was like trying to stop a steamroller. Ty sat back with a sigh. "Yes?"

"Client?"

"Olsen Associates. Venture capital fund. Based in New York. Registered in the Caymans. Mr. Lane's part of a three-man office in Budapest covering Eastern Europe from Poland in the west to the former Soviet Republic of Latvia in the east. They have diverse interests, but their Budapest office is mostly focused on energy and agriculture. Lane was primarily tasked with finding new investment opportunities." Ty stopped. "Anything else, or can I go hit the head?"

Lock nodded him to go ahead and watched as Ty sprang from his seat to go flirt at the bar with the blonde cabin crew member. Lock turned his attention back to the file in front of him. He flicked to the section that profiled the kidnappers. Precise details were scarce but from the profile gathered from a number of local sources it looked like a small to medium-sized organized crime crew had stumbled into the kidnap-for-ransom business. It also appeared that this wasn't their first rodeo. This was the third Western businessman targeted by Budapest-based organized crime gangs in the past six months.

In cases like this, and with corruption still being a feature of life in modern Hungary, the decision had been taken to simply pay the negotiated sum and move on. After all, that was why international companies took out K and R (kidnap for ransom) insurance. Apart from those immediately involved no one would ever know. If the cops in Hungary wanted to deal with it after his release, that would be up to them. But right now the only thing that mattered was Mr. Lane's safe return to London.

Lock flipped to the next page. He took a sip of mineral water. If all went to plan he'd be back in this seat, with a glass of champagne in his hand in under forty eight hours.

3

András Szarka, the negotiation team's designated communicator, stared at the phone ringing on the table. An earnest newcomer to the world of conflict resolution, with a rock climber's wiry frame and an easy smile, he put on his headset, and waited, counting off the seconds. He already knew who would be on the other end of the line. The only people who had the number were the kidnappers. When precisely five seconds had passed, he picked it up.

"This is András," he said in Hungarian.

Around the conference table, the two other people present, all with headphones connected to the phone, listened intently to the voice on the other end of the line. No one else spoke. They were running silent now. Only András had a headset with a microphone. Next to him, his boss, the chief negotiator, a Scottish psychologist by the name of James Robertson, scribbled a note and slid it over the desk to András.

András glanced at the note, and gave Robertson a thumbs up. "No," he said to the man on the other end of the line, "we agreed two hundred forty six thousand, and five hundred US dollars. I'd also remind you that it comes with a commitment from you that there will be no further targeting of any other Olsen Associates employees or anyone linked to them, either here in Hungary or anywhere else. Call us back when you have the exchange details."

Robertson's thumb turned downwards, a pre-arranged signal that they had used in a number of previous instances. András ended the call. The line went dead.

Chairs slid back from the conference table. András shot his boss a look. Robertson returned it with a smile.

"Don't worry, they'll call back. Do we have a stopwatch on it?" Robertson asked the dark-haired woman sitting next to him. Yuksia Vertov, another local, was the negotiation team's coordinator. She held up her iPhone. The stopwatch function was already running.

Last minute re-negotiations were not uncommon. In this case, the original demand had been five million dollars. Robertson had dismissed that out of hand, countering with an offer of twenty thousand dollars. The kidnappers had blown a gasket, as he knew they would. Twenty thousand was as absurd as their demand. That was the point of it.

The kidnappers had huffed and puffed for some considerable time. They had called back and screamed abuse at András. Listening in, Robertson may not have known the precise terms being used, but there was no mistaking the displeasure.

Once he'd had András patiently explain to the kidnap gang that the brokers at Lloyds in London who had underwritten the K and R insurance policy for Olsen Associates were not about to pay out five million dollars to a mid-sized Hungarian organized crime gang, negotiations settled down. In the background, Robertson used his considerable experience of such cases to balance the need to get Michael home safe as quickly as possible with the most powerful weapon in a negotiation – escalation of commitment.

Time may have been something the kidnappers could use, but it cut both ways. The longer the negotiation, the more invested the kidnappers were in seeing some money at the end of it. Even a single hostage had to be guarded around the clock. Guards, even ones already on the pay roll, were still a cost that had to be applied against income. The longer the kidnap period ran for, the higher the cost to their organization. The higher the cost, the lower their final profit.

Yuksia tapped the red stop button on her iPhone screen as the phone rang. The display read two minutes, thirty four seconds, and ninety nine hundredths of a second. András waited for Robertson's signal before answering.

"You are a bitch, András! Your mother is also a bitch! You are a son of a bitch."

András rolled his eyes. "You may be correct, but what did you call to tell me?"

He looked over at Robertson, checking his boss's reaction for signs of a rebuke. András liked to freestyle. Robertson allowed him some latitude, but occasionally he would over-step the mark. This time was fine though. Barring last minute complications, this was a straight up case. They were criminals. They wanted money and the hostage off their hands. It was business, regardless of the man on the line questioning the communicator's lineage.

"You pay the full amount you offered, yes?" said the kidnapper.

András looked over at Robertson. Robertson gave him the thumbs up. "Yes, of course. We're honorable people. Now what about the exchange?"

"We will call you tomorrow to make the arrangements. Be ready."

This time they allowed the kidnapper to end the call. Let them have their moment. Yuksia looked up from her iPhone. "The exchange team just landed in London. Flight was on time. I told them to meet us here."

4

The negotiation team's base was a suite at the Gresham Four Seasons, a five star hotel on the banks of Danube, with a jaw-dropping view of the city's iconic Chain Bridge. In a city with some very good hotels, the Gresham was the most opulent. The rooms were luxurious. The service was impeccable. To people for whom money was no object, this was the only place to stay in the Hungarian capital.

Lock and Ty stepped out of the private car arranged by the hotel's concierge. A doorman ushered them into the lobby of the Art Noveau building. The lobby had as much in common with a regular hotel reception as a beat up Chevy pick-up truck had with a Ferrari. The centerpiece was an ornate chandelier made up of hundreds of glass leaves. Staring up at it, Ty looked almost as impressed as he had been with the cute young flight attendant he'd finally gotten a number from on their flight to London.

Lock didn't blame Ty for his slack-jawed expression. Lock rarely did these types of gigs, but when he did he always wondered why he didn't do more of them. They could be nerve-shredding, but the perks, including the hotels, were almost always excellent.

The reason was two-fold. Five star hotels usually came with a certain level of in-built security and the first rule of a hostage situation was not to become one yourself. Additionally, an insurer paying a quarter of a million dollar ransom tended not to nickel and dime the personnel making sure they got what they were paying for on time and in one piece. Lock and Ty were known on The Circuit, the informal web of private security companies and contacts that had burgeoned since 9/11, as reliable operators.

Lock's phone buzzed with an incoming text. He read it as the receptionist took their details and arranged the key cards for their rooms. As Lock read the text, Ty shooed away an over-eager bellhop who wanted to take their bags. Ty politely explained that the bags were staying with them. The bellhop retreated with a deferential nod.

Lock put his cell back in his pocket and stepped away from the desk so that he could talk to Ty without being overheard. "We're meeting the team in a half hour for an initial briefing. Then it's dinner at the restaurant here and then an early night. Tomorrow should be pick-up day. We have three seats booked on the last flight back to London. That's the good news."

Ty frowned. "What's the bad news?"

"The last flight out of Budapest is operated by an airline called Ryanair."

"Why's that bad news?" asked Ty.

"You'll figure it out. But don't worry, we're business class back to Los Angeles on Monday morning," Lock said, turning back to the strikingly beautiful young brunette behind the reception desk.

THEY TOOK the elevator up to the fourth floor. They had been given rooms next to each other. Lock left Ty to get unpacked, opened the door into his room and walked in. He dumped his bag on the floor, and walked to the window. The bridge was lit up. The lights reflected off the murky black waters of the Danube. Across the river he could make out the hilly slopes of the Buda side of the city. The street below was empty, the bitter cold having driven people inside. Thick gray clouds overhead threatened snow.

Lock closed the drapes, walked back into the room and flicked on the lights. On the bed was a black gun case, his welcome present, arranged by the negotiating team, per his request. He flipped it open to reveal a brand new SIG Sauer P229 with three fifteen round magazines. He didn't foresee having to use it, but the people they were dealing with were hardly boy scouts. It was better to be prepared for all eventualities.

He took the 229 from the case, and checked it over. Robertson had estimated that they'd transfer the cash by electronic transfer in the morning, and then collect the package in the late afternoon. That would give Lock time to head to a nearby range in the morning and fire some rounds. The car and driver they'd be using would be parked outside, ready to deploy them as soon as the call came. Spending time at the range would beat waiting around at the hotel with the others.

Lock unpacked quickly. He placed his body armor vest on a hanger in the wardrobe, and laid out his dark gray Hugo Boss suit, fresh underwear, and a clean white shirt. He secured the hotel room door and took a quick shower, scrubbing off travel grime. He dried off, got dressed, left the SIG in the room safe, set up another small motion activated camera next to a desk lamp as a precautionary measure, and left the room.

He caught up with Ty at the elevator. Ty was wearing slacks and a sport coat, which was about as dressed up as he got. "You get your present?" Lock asked him, hitting the button to take them back down to the ground floor.

"Sure did," Ty said. "Box fresh. We get to keep them once we're done here?"

Lock thought it over for a moment. "I can ask Robertson if he'll ship them."

The elevator slowed and then stopped at the second floor. The doors opened to reveal Robertson. He was flanked by a young man in his twenties whom Lock assumed was the team's communicator, András. To Robertson's left was a young woman of similar age whose looks were like a dictionary definition of the phrase 'jaw dropping.'

Lock wasn't sure what he'd been expecting Yuksia Vertov to look like. All he knew was that he hadn't expected this.

Next to him, Ty's tongue was threatening to roll out of his mouth. Lock quickly reminded himself that they were here for a short time and not a good time. He shook hands with Robertson.

"Impeccable timing," said Robertson, stepping into the elevator and making the introductions.

Lock shook hands with András. When it came time to shake hands with Yuksia, she held his gaze, as well as his hand, a little longer than was necessary. "So you are the famous Ryan Lock," she said in a softly accented voice. "James has told us many stories."

Lock tried to think of a snappy come back but came up blank. The elevator doors opened. She dropped her hand from his.

"After you," said Lock, ushering her out ahead of them. She smiled, turned, and walked ahead with András, leaving Lock to talk to Robertson as they walked the short distance across the hotel lobby to the Gresham restaurant. Ty had caught up to the two young Hungarians and was running his usual game on Yuksia.

"How was your flight?" Robertson asked.

"Very pleasant. Oh, and thanks for the welcome gift," said Lock, referencing the two SIG 229s.

Robertson held up his hands, palms open. "Those are off the books. Nothing to do with me. Not officially in any case. But I figured that as these people are an unknown quantity, you might feel more comfortable carrying."

As the maître d' ushered them to a circular table at the back of the long room, Robertson nodded to the street outside. "Budapest is hardly the wild west, but I guess they have their problems with organized crime like everyone else."

"So what do you think went down?" Lock asked Robertson. "I mean a KR case involving a British national in Eastern Europe doesn't fit the usual profile."

They took their seats, Lock next to Robertson. Across the table, Yuksia seemed to be studying him. It made concentrating on what Robertson was saying abnormally difficult. She had long, soft, chestnut hair, with eyes to match, and bone structure that would make a supermodel envious.

"You have to remember, Ryan, that most KR cases are quietly settled without anyone being any the wiser. But you're correct, this isn't a typical case," Robertson said.

Lock took a menu from the waiter. They ordered water for the table. The waiter melted back into the background.

"So," said Lock. "Why this guy?"

"My job doesn't involve the whys," Robertson said. "I'm not a cop. I'm simply here to make sure that Michael gets back home safely and to minimize the ransom payment. But if I had to make a guess I'd say it was a simple case of opportunity. You say the wrong thing to the wrong person, or flash your money somewhere you shouldn't, and voilà, all of a sudden the wrong kind of people take an interest in you."

"So who do you think he ran into?" pressed Lock.

Robertson pursed his lips. "No idea."

"You're not curious?" Lock asked.

Across the table, Yuksia was still studying him with a quiet intensity. Part of him was already hoping that the transfer would hit a non-fatal snag and he'd get a few more days in Budapest.

Robertson pressed his fingertips together, the gesture giving away a hint of the academic he'd been before he'd realized he could make ten times the money in the private sector actually resolving conflicts rather than telling others how they should resolve them. "My being curious isn't going to help Michael Lane get back home. I'd say that once we do the de-brief with him we may be able to work out who set him up, assuming that's what happened. Then again, we may never know. Anyway, this isn't part of your remit either." He half-turned in his seat. "Why do you care?"

Lock wasn't about to go into it at dinner. "Would you happen to have a key to Lane's apartment?"

"Why would you want to take a look at the man's apartment?" said Robertson.

Lock shrugged. "It's probably nothing, but there was something in the report that I'd like to check on. Like I said, it's probably nothing."

Robertson smiled. "Well, I think Yuksia has a set of keys. I'm sure she can arrange access for you. You want to go after dinner? I don't think you'll have time tomorrow."

Lock glanced across at the table. "Maybe I should leave it."

Robertson waved him away. "Yuksia?"

She glanced across at the two men as the waiter returned to take their order. "Would you mind showing Mr.. Lock Michael Lane's apartment?"

"Of course," she said. "It would be my pleasure."

5

The sudden exposure to light made Michael Lane wince. The headache that had sat sullenly in the middle of his skull for the past few days flared up. Looking down he saw the same dirty, bare floor boards. His backside was numb from sitting in the same position for too long. He had pins and needles in his legs. His lower back ached, and he was hungry.

Narrowing his eyes, he looked up at the hulking figure standing over him. In one hand, the man held the blindfold he had just removed. In his other hand was a suit carrier. He laid the carrier down on the bed in the corner of the room. He walked behind Michael and untied the short length of rope around his wrists. Finally, he helped Michael to his feet.

Michael caught a whiff of garlicky body odor. His stomach lurched. A huge hand clamped around his bicep and the man led him towards the small en-suite bathroom.

He was usually allowed a shower every day or every second day. It depended on which of the four regular guards were on duty. The biggest of them, the one he was with now, usually avoided letting him shower. Michael guessed it was because it required extra effort on his part, and the guard was lazy.

As Michael's eyes adjusted to the light from a bare lightbulb overhead, he saw something different lying at the edge of the sink. It was an old fashioned safety razor - the kind that used regular razor blades. Next to it was a can of shaving foam. When he was allowed to shave it was usually with a cheap, plastic disposable razor.

The guard pointed at the shower and then at his new shaving kit. The gesture was accompanied by a grunt. The guard turned and walked out of the bathroom, leaving Michael alone.

Michael stood there for a moment. He stared at himself in the mirror. He had dark patches under his eyes. His skin was pale and oily. What muscle tone he'd had was gone. He was skinny-fat from a lack of exercise (before he was kidnapped he would run along the Danube most mornings and hit the gym after work), and the constant stream of heavy Hungarian food and sweets he was fed. One thing he hadn't been able to accuse his captors of was starving him. At times he had felt like a turkey being fattened for Thanksgiving. Judging by the suit carrier and the safety razor it looked like Thanksgiving had finally arrived and he was going to be freed.

There was only one problem. He didn't want to put back on a plane to London. Not yet anyway. At least not until he knew she was safe.

6

It was close to eleven o'clock by the time Yuksia's Skoda Fabia car pulled up outside Michael Lane's apartment on Hild Ter in Budapest's District 5. Despite being talkative at dinner, as soon as Yuksia had got into her car with Lock, she had gone quiet. As she drove the short distance from the Four Seasons to the apartment she would sneak glances at him under the pretext of checking the traffic in her rearview and side mirrors.

Once she had squeezed the Fabia into a parking spot, she fished in her handbag for the set of keys to the apartment. As she handed them to Lock her fingertips brushed against his open palm. They looked at each other for a little longer than was comfortable. Lock's hand closed around the keys and she looked away. Whatever temporary spell that had fallen between them was broken.

"Would you like me to come with you?" Yuksia asked him.

From an operational point of view it didn't matter whether she accompanied him or stayed in the car. "Always good to have another pair of eyes," said Lock, getting out of the car.

Yuksia joined him on the sidewalk. The street was quiet. While Yuksia was wearing the same dress she'd had on for dinner, Lock had changed into jeans, sneakers, a sweatshirt, and slightly over-sized black wind breaker that concealed the shoulder holster that was holding his SIG 229. He had caught Yuksia sneaking a glance at the gun as he got out of the car.

They stood together at the heavy metal and glass doors that led into the foyer of the apartment building. Lock worked his way through the two keys on the key ring until he found the one that opened the door. He pushed through, Yuksia close enough behind him that he could smell her perfume.

The elevator was an antique affair with a manually operated metal grille door. Lock hauled it open. Yuksia stepped in. He joined her inside and hit the button to take them to the third floor.

The elevator juddered into life. Yuksia gave a nervous laugh. It was a slow journey up. They would have been quicker taking the stairs. Lock didn't mind. They both defaulted to standard elevator behavior by staring straight ahead in silence. The only thing that was different was how comfortable he felt with the silence and her standing next to him. He glanced over at her. She smiled and looked away. He had to remind himself that he was here on business.

Finally, they reached the third floor with another grating shudder. Lock hauled open the two metal grilles and they stepped out into the corridor. Lock opened the door into the apartment and stepped inside. Yuksia followed.

The building may not have looked much from the street but the apartment was pretty impressive. The main area was a thousand square foot kitchen/dining area/living room. There was a bathroom and two large bedrooms, each with their own en-suite bathroom. The furniture was sleek and contemporary. Large canvases of brightly colored modern art adorned the walls. There was a large flatscreen television on the far wall, and a 5K Retina iMac on a desk in the corner.

Lock began the search in the kitchen. He opened the refrigerator before moving onto drawers and cupboards.

"What are you looking for?" Yuksia asked him.

Lock stopped. He glanced up from a drawer full of knives. "What I always look for. The absence of the normal. The presence of the abnormal."

He moved through into the master bedroom. Yuksia followed. Lock crossed to a dresser and began opening drawers and rifling through the contents. "What would you expect to find in the apartment of a married man living on his own?"

Yuksia shrugged. "I don't know."

Lock closed the final drawer. "Porn on the computer? A little too much alcohol? Maybe some drugs if he's working long hours in a high-pressure environment like finance? Coke, uppers, Modafinil to keep him focussed and on top of his game."

Lock threw open a wardrobe. He slid back the hangars with Michael Lane's suits and shirts. Nothing. He reached down to open the first of two lower drawers. He stopped, and plucked out a piece of skimpy black lingerie. He dug further down and came up with more flimsy pieces of silk material

"Either Michael Lane was a cross dresser? Or maybe he had company the morning he was kidnapped?" he said.

"Maybe his wife left them here after a visit?" Yuksia offered.

Lock checked the size tag on the back of a lacy red bra. At least he thought it was a bra, but he couldn't be sure. The size tag made up about a quarter of the entire surface area. "There's picture of Lane's wife in the file. She's an attractive woman, but believe me, these don't belong to her. And the size of these also kind of rules out my first theory that he might like to slip into something a little more comfortable when he gets home. The only thing he'd be able to use this for would be dental floss."

Yuksia walked over to him. She plucked the bra from his hands and held it up to her chest. "He was having an affair. So what?"

Lock took the piece of skimpy material back and threw it back into the drawer. "The 'so what' is that kidnap victims tend not to be picked out of thin air. There's reason to believe that the other Western businessmen who've been kidnapped here had gotten involved with local women. At least that was alluded to in the report. I think Michael Lane was the victim of a honeytrap."

Yuksia's brow furrowed. "A honeytrap? I don't know this word."

"The gang uses an attractive younger woman to get closer to the vic. That way they can gather information on him and his company. It's a hell of a lot easier than following him or hacking his computer."

"Perhaps if men weren't so easily led," said Yuksia.

Lock ignored that one. He walked into the master bathroom. He opened the cabinet. Among the bottles of shampoo and conditioner and a can of shaving foam was a pack of pink lady's disposable razors. In the medicine cabinet above the sink he found a pack of blue Cialis erectile dysfunction pills. Michael Lane was young and in good physical shape. Lock doubted he'd need them for anything other than recreational use.

Walking back out into the main bedroom, Yuksia had discovered a knee length black cocktail dress stuffed into a bag at the back of the wardrobe. She held it up against her body, modeling it for him. Not that Lock endorsed infidelity but if the woman Michael had been seeing looked half as good as the young Hungarian woman standing in front of him now, Lock could at least understand the temptation.

7

Michael stood under the limp trickle of lukewarm water and unscrewed the handle of the double edged safety razor. He lifted off the top part of the head, and gently levered out the razor blade. Stepping out of the shower, he laid the blade down on the edge of the sink, and screwed the head back into the razor's handle. He left the water running while he quickly dried off and changed into the new clothes he'd just been given.

Rolling up his right shirt sleeve, he reached in and shut the water off. He crossed back to the sink, and slid the razor blade to the edge where he could pick it up. He held it between the thumb and index finger of his right hand. He let his hand fall to his side as he looked at himself in the mirror. His heart was racing. He took a couple of deep breaths.

There was a knock at the bathroom door. He startled.

"I'm almost done," he said.

It was now or never. If it was going to work he would have to do it as soon as the door opened. He would reach up and slash at the side of the guard's neck. The razor was fresh out of the packet. It wouldn't take any pressure at all to cut the man's jugular vein.

Another knock. "Okay! Okay!" Michael shouted.

One last deep breath. One final look at himself in the mirror. Portrait of a man before he becomes a murderer. He could already see it unfold in his mind's eye. The arc of his hand. The blade slicing through flesh. The first pulse of blood. The look of surprise on the bigger man's face as he realized what had just happened.

Michael reached out with his left hand and opened the bathroom door.

There was no one there. The room appeared to be empty. He stepped through the door. The razor blade was still pinched between his thumb and index finger.

It was only then that he saw the guard. He had pulled the chair into the corner of the room. He was sitting on it, facing Michael, a matt black gun in his hand. The barrel pointed straight at Michael's chest. The guard's free hand reached up to rub his own face.

"Can I help you with something?" said the guard.

Michael could hear the sound of his blood pumping in his ears. The guard was staring at his right hand. "You speak English," he said, dumbfounded. Not once had he heard any of the guards speak anything other than Hungarian.

The guard smiled. "You forgot to shave."

"I forgot," said Michael, trying to force himself to smile at the man. "I'll do it now."

The guard grinned at him. He nodded towards Michael's right hand. "Put the blade back in the razor. Don't be silly again, Michael. You are going home."

"But what about Katya?" said Michael, his voice cracking.

The guard dissolved into a gale of laughter. "Katya?"

Michael's jaw tightened with anger. "Yes, Katya."

The guard had to struggle to stop laughing. "Katya is fine, Michael. Believe me on this."

Michael walked back into the bathroom. He started to close the door.

"Leave it open," the guard said.

Michael did as he was told. He crossed back to the sink and picked up the safety razor. The guard watched with a smile as Michael put the blade back in the head.

8

Lock got into the front passenger seat of Yuksia's car. She sat there, staring silently up at the windows of the apartment. She glanced back over at Lock with big, brown eyes. "Are you always this suspicious?" she asked him, pushing back a stray strand of hair that had fallen over her right cheek

He thought about it for a moment, turning the question over in his mind. He couldn't exactly say no, but saying yes didn't seem like an adequate answer either. "Let's just say that I don't believe in coincidences."

Yuksia started the engine, and pulled away from the curb. "I agree with you." She snuck a glance at him as made a sharp left, heading down a side street and back towards the river and Lock's hotel. "Everything happens for a reason."

They were driving next to the river. The Chain Bridge was up ahead, its lights shimmering in the moonlight. Suddenly, Yuksia pulled the car over to the side of the road. She put on the parking brake and slammed her hands down onto the steering wheel. "Let's go for a walk," she announced, getting out of the car before Lock could protest.

"I thought you were taking me back to the hotel," said Lock joining her on the sidewalk.

She waved her hand down the street. "It's right there. You can go to your room. Or you can take a walk with me. It's up to you."

He wasn't going to sleep. He already knew that. He had too much churning around his head. Michael Lane. Who the woman he'd met was and where, if anywhere, she fitted into his abduction. Whether the other men who had been kidnapped had also fallen for the same subterfuge. And, if he was being honest with himself, his mind would also be on Yuksia who had already slipped her hand into his, and was pulling him gently towards the bridge.

"We can go look at the castle on the other side of the river," she said.

She wasn't leaving him with too many options. Plus, walking hand in hand with a pretty young woman after midnight next to the Danube wasn't the worst thing that had happened to him. There wasn't too much by way of preparations that he could make for the exchange. By its very nature they would have no idea about the collection point until the very last second, so reconnaissance would be a pointless exercise.

As they reached the bridge's footpath they passed a stone lion mounted on a plinth. Its partner was on the other side of the road, both lions seemingly guarding the mouth of the bridge. Yuksia's hand felt warm and comforting in Lock's.

"You grew up here?" Lock asked her.

"Yes," she said. "On the Buda side of the river. That's where the prettiest girls are from."

Lock laughed. "Oh, really?"

She looked up at him with a frown. "Yes, really. What about you? Where do you live?"

"All depends on where work takes me. Los Angeles. New York. Here today. Then London tomorrow. Then back to LA, I guess. Unless I get a call while I'm in London that takes me somewhere else."

They stopped for a moment and took in the grand sweep of the buildings on either side of the Danube. Yuksia pointed out some of the main landmarks to him from the Gothic Revival majesty of the Hungarian Parliament building on the Pest side to the brooding baroque Castle that sat high on the Buda side. It really was a beautiful city, thought Lock.

"Doesn't your girlfriend get upset that you are always traveling?" Yuksia asked him as they began walking again.

"You're fishing," said Lock.

"Fishing?"

He shook his head. "Doesn't matter. I don't have a girlfriend. It wouldn't be fair to get involved with someone with the life I have."

They were reaching the other side of the river. "Do you mind if I ask you something personal?" Yuksia said.

Lock shrugged. He had a feeling she would ask anyway. She was refreshingly direct.

"Don't get offended okay," she said.

"I don't offend easily," said Lock.

"You like women?" Yuksia said.

Lock burst out laughing. He couldn't help it. "You think I'm gay?" he said with a broad grin.

"I don't want to make a fool of myself," she said.

Lock turned towards her with a smile. He leaned down and kissed her on the lips. She kissed him back. His hand touched her face, brushing away the hair as he kissed her once more, more deeply this time. She snuggled in closer, her hands settling around his waist. After a few more kisses, he pulled back a little.

"I'm leaving tomorrow," Lock said.

She reached down and took his hand. "I'm not a child. I do know that. But perhaps if you really don't believe in coincidences we should go to your room. It's a better place to see the castle from."

"You want to go to my room for a better view of the castle?" he said.

She shrugged. "Yes, of course. Why else?"

9

They were less than four hundred yards from the hotel entrance when Lock heard a car accelerating behind them. He half turned. Out of the corner of his eye, he saw a dark sedan driving towards them. The rear nearside window glided down. The long barrel of a gun penetrated the gap.

Lock wrapped around an arm around Yuksia and pushed her down onto the sidewalk. With his right hand he reached in under his jacket, and pulled out the SIG 229. Lying on top of Yuksia, he heard the rapid chatter of bullets flying over his head.

He looked up. The car was still moving slowly past them. It came to a stop and whipped round, headed back for another try. This time Lock was ready. The attackers' element of surprise was gone.

Using his knees and elbows, he crawled over Yuksia, placing his body between her and the gun car. Staying low, he took aim at the front windshield, aiming for the driver's side about a foot above the hood. Even if the driver was hunkered down, they'd still need some kind of a visual. If they weren't hunched over the steering wheel then, with a little luck, he'd catch them flush in the chest.

Using less pressure on the second shot, he fired. The round went a little high. It punched through the windshield. The sedan braked. The driver threw it into neutral and began to back up. Lock fire twice more. Both shots punched through the windshield.

The driver spun the wheel, making another turn. Lock fired a fourth round at the car as it sped away into the night. He could hear sirens in the distance. He had no idea if they were headed towards them, but he wasn't about to take any chances. He was carrying a gun he wasn't legally entitled to have in his possession, in a foreign country where the cops weren't entirely dependable. He got to his feet and reached down to help Yuksia.

"You okay?" he said.

She was gasping for air but that was likely hyperventilation from the shock. Lock jammed his SIG back into his holster and zipped up his jacket. He took a firm grip of Yuksia's hand and walked her briskly across the street towards the hotel entrance as if they were merely continuing their romantic midnight stroll. Down the street a small group of late night revelers stared at them. Lock ignored them and kept walking with Yuksia.

It was only when they hit the brightly lit lobby that he turned round. A police car whipped past on the street outside. He steered Yuksia towards the elevator. The elevator doors opened. He bundled her inside, his hand on the arch of her back. He hit the button to take them to the floor above his room. He hadn't seen anyone watching them in the lobby but he didn't want to take any chance of someone following them to his room. They would walk back down one flight of stairs.

Yuksia's breathing had slowed. He dropped her hand, and brushed away the strands of rich chestnut hair that had fallen across her face. There was a dark smudge across her right cheek where she had made contact with the sidewalk.

"You in any pain?" he asked her.

She shook her head. "I don't think so."

The elevator stopped. Lock lowered the zip on his jacket a few inches so that he had easier access to the SIG if he needed to pull it again. The elevator doors opened. He led Yuksia towards the stair-well. They walked briskly down the stairs.

As they emerged back into the corridor, Ty was standing outside Lock's room. He saw Lock and turned towards them. "What's going on? There's like half a dozen cop cars out front and I heard a bunch of shots. I thought this was a nice neighborhood too. Four Seasons and shit."

Lock raised his finger to his lips, shushing Ty. He opened the door into his room and led Yuksia inside. Ty followed. Lock kept the lights off. He closed the door behind them.

The three of them stood in the gloom. Lock walked to the window. Down on the street a dozen cop cars had now assembled. Uniformed and plainclothes officers stood in clusters. A couple were shining their torches, no doubt looking for shell casings and broken glass.

Ty was already rifling the room's mini-bar. He poured Yuksia a Scotch and handed it to her. She took it with trembling hands.

"You want anything?" he asked Lock. "They got that Toblerone chocolate up in here. Already ate the one I had in my room."

Lock couldn't help but smile at the object of Ty's focus. He had been seconds from being killed in a drive-by and his partner's main interest was almond and honey-infused chocolate.

Ty fished the chocolate bar from the small fridge and began to open it. "Okay, well your loss. These are really good." He sliced the foil with his thumbnail, broke off a triangle and offered it to Yuksia. When she shook her head, he popped the triangle into his mouth. "So what was that about?" he asked Lock, with a nod towards the window.

Lock shrugged. "No idea. Yuksia was showing me the castle. We were just walking back to the hotel when those chumps drove past and tried a pop and drop."

"You get a look at them?" said Ty.

"Nope," said Lock, "and even if I had I'm not sure what good it would have done. I'm not really familiar with Budapest's Most

Wanted. What do you think, Yuksia? You get many random drive-bys here?"

She shook her head, and finished the rest of the Scotch. She dug in the bar for a refill, twisted off the small cap, tossed into a nearby waste basket and poured another measure into her glass. "Like you said. There's no such thing as a coincidence."

10

Lock had never thought that gunfire might be an aphrodisiac. He'd been wrong. As soon as things had settled down, the cops had dispersed, and Ty had gone to his own room, Lock had gone to take a shower, leaving Yuksia to finish her whisky. Lock always found the shower a good place to decompress, and think things over. There was something about the steady drumbeat of the water and the heat that relaxed him.

For security reasons he had kept the door slightly ajar so that if anyone came into the room he would see be able to see them in the bathroom mirror. Instead what he saw was Yuksia's dress drop to the floor, and her step out of it. Next her bra and panties came off. There was a little more in the way of material than the underwear they'd found at Michael Lane's apartment, but not much. Maybe there was a worldwide silk and lace shortage that Lock hadn't read about in the Wall Street Journal.

Yuksia opened the bathroom door and stood staring at him. Her figure was sensational. Toned and curvy in just the right proportions. She'd tied her hair back in a ponytail at some point, giving Lock a good view of her full, soft breasts. She moved with grace and confidence towards the shower, and opened the door. Lock took a step back. She reached up and put her arms around his shoulders. He bent down a little and kissed her. Her lips parted. Her tongue slid inside his mouth. Her passion was raw and immediate. She wrapped herself around him, reaching one had down to stroke the inside of his thigh. He stared into her eyes, losing himself in her as she took hold him.

Lock's hands slid down her back. He cupped her ass cheeks, and lifted her up. Her legs wrapped around his waist as he lowered her onto him, the water pounding down onto them from the powerful shower head.

Yuksia ran her fingers through his hair. Her hands went lower, her nails digging into his back with increasing ferocity as she rode on top of him. He eased up, not wanting it to end too fast. He turned so that her back was against the tiled wall. With her arms around his neck, he let her make the pace, lifting and lowering her onto him as she demanded. Her breath quickened. He felt her tighten around him. She let out a cry and bit down on her lower lip. Her head tilted back as she came. He lowered her slowly so that he was deep inside her. He let her have the moment.

Her eyes opened. "Take me to bed."

Lock's powerful arms hoisted her up even higher. He slipped out of her and held her, one arm under her legs, the other supporting her back. He nudged the shower door open with his foot, and carried her back through into the bedroom.

Outside, the street was quiet as he laid Yuksia gently down onto the kingsized bed.

11

———

The next morning, Lock left Yuksia to get ready and made his way down to breakfast in the hotel's Gresham restaurant. Ty was already busy working his way through most of the lengthy breakfast menu, while Robertson and András looked on in wonderment. Lock slid into a seat next to his business partner as Ty finished a plate of pancakes and moved onto eggs and sausage. A waiter made the rounds with coffee and fresh water. He too looked in awe at the carnage. Ty took a slurp of coffee and shot Lock a grin.

"You got that look about you, brother."

Lock knew that asking 'what look' would be a fatal mistake. "How was your Toblerone?"

Ty's grin grew broader. "Delicious. How was yours?"

Lock ignored him and turned to Robertson. "Michael Lane was having an affair. Almost certainly with someone he met when he moved here. I think she may be the key to why he was targeted."

While András looked shocked, Robertson didn't react. His hands smoothed out the napkin on his lap. "I'll report that back. But today's game day. We should get the details of where they want the money transferred to this morning."

"They don't want cash?" Lock asked.

Robertson smiled. "Not these days. Times change. I handled a K and R case last month in Venezuela where the kidnappers insisted on being paid in Bitcoin via a darkweb site. Dropping cash leaves them way too exposed."

"Okay," said Lock. "So all we have to do is collect our package?"

"Correct," said Robertson. "I've arranged a car with a driver and Yuksia can navigate for you. She knows the city like the back of her hand."

"Bet that's not the only thing she knows like the back of her hand," muttered Ty with a side-long smile at Lock.

"Speak of the devil," said András.

Lock looked up to see Yuksia walking towards them. She looked stunning. Her skin glowed, only to flush a little as she made eye contact with him. Lock stood up and pulled out a seat.

"Thank you," she said, the picture of innocence.

"I was just telling Ryan that you can help handle the navigation to the collection point," said Robertson.

"Of course," said Yuksia. "It would be my pleasure."

Ty choked back a laugh. "Good eggs," he said, stabbing his fork at another freshly cleaned plate. "What a great city. Huh, Ryan?"

"Did you hear about what happened last night when Yuksia was bringing me back here?" Lock asked Robertson.

The Scottish negotiator took a sip of coffee. "Worrying. I'm not sure quite what to make of it. It couldn't be random. Not here."

"So what do you think?" pressed Lock. "Why would a kidnap gang take a shot at someone who's going to be giving them a bunch of money?"

Lock noticed András studiously staring at the table cloth before taking a slug of coffee. Robertson shrugged. "They probably want to keep it as just business. You poking round Lane's apartment takes it into slightly different territory. Or maybe I'm reading too much into it. Either way, let's be on our guard today. If there's anything else you need before you deploy then let me know." He stood up. "I'd better check in with the broker in London. Make sure we're all set for the transfer on our end. That's scheduled for eleven am. András spoke to them last night and they indicated they'd release Michael as soon as the funds were cleared into their offshore account."

Ty looked up from his plate. "We give them the money first?"

"Simultaneous exchanges are extremely rare," said Robertson. "Apart from in the movies. The usual deal is money first then they release the package into our care."

Lock and Ty exchanged a look. "Doesn't that mean they could just kill Michael Lane?"

Robertson cleared his throat. He had the professorial air of a man who had grown accustomed to having just this conversation. "They could. But that would destroy any repeat business and bring down a lot of heat of them. Generally, unless you are dealing with jihadists or other political groups, kidnappers treat it as business. It's bad business to kill someone after you've been paid. These guys may be relatively new to this, but they'll understand that."

"Still seems like a risk to me," Ty said, pushing his plate away unfinished.

Robertson rested his elbows on the table, and pressed his fingertips together. "I've dealt with coming up on fifty K and R negotiations. Out of all of those cases I've only once had a hostage killed after the ransom was paid. And that was because they lost patience, did something stupid and attempted to escape before the exchange team got to them."

"So," said Lock. "Your advice would be for us not to be late and to stop sticking our nose where it doesn't belong."

"I wouldn't put it quite that bluntly," Robertson said. "But that would be the gist of it."

12

Lock handed Yuksia his SIG P299, a round already in the chamber. He stepped back as she took up a Weaver stance and began to fire the first of the fifteen rounds in the magazine. She handled the recoil no problem, adjusting her aim slightly with each shot, and finishing with two tight clusters. The first cluster centered in the chest of the silhouette target. The second cluster of shots punched through the inverted triangle marked out in the center of the target's head.

She ejected the empty magazine and laid the gun down on the bench. Next to it, her cell phone flashed with an incoming text message from Robertson. She picked up her cell, opened the message and palmed it to Lock so that he could read it.

The money transfer had been cleared and verified by the kidnappers. András had just taken the call. The kidnappers were ready to release the package. They were going to call with a location in a half hour. With no clue as to where it might be, Lock, Ty and Yuksia were to sit tight, ready to deploy at a moment's notice.

Lock had met with the original driver that had been lined up after breakfast. He was middle-aged, a former city cop who smelled of stale beer and onions. He had the death pallor and yellow-edged eyes of a man whose first waking thought was of where his first drink was coming from. Lock wouldn't have let him drive a bumper car at a fairground, never mind handle transport on a live operation.

With a last minute alternative hard to come and the clock ticking, Lock suggested that he drive the car while Yuksia navigated. Ty had shot him a look, which Lock had ignored. He did want to spend what little time they had left with her, but she was also a good fit for the job. Her English was impeccable, she had been calmer than most people under live fire, and he trusted her. She could also, from what he'd just seen, handle a gun if called upon to do so.

Ty strolled down from his lane at the opposite end of the range. His SIG P229 was holstered. He stood next to Lock as he inserted a fresh clip into his weapon, racked the slide, and holstered it.

"We good to go?" Ty asked Yuksia.

"Soon," said Yuksia. "Shall we walk out to the car?"

Together, the three of them thanked the owner of the gun range, and strolled out past the reception area, down the long winding corridor, and out into the fresh early afternoon sunshine. It was cold but clear with blue skies overhead. Yuksia gave Lock to the keys her car and he climbed into the driver's seat, pushing the seat back to adjust for his larger frame. Ty's long legs meant he claimed shotgun. Yuksia climbed in back. Just as she settled herself in her seat, her cell phone chirped with a fresh text message.

Lock studied her puzzled reaction as she scanned the message. "Problem?" he asked her.

"They want us to go to the zoo."

Next to Lock, Ty struggled to half-turn in his seat. "Say what?"

Yuksia held up the cell phone so he could read the message. "They want us to drive to Budapest Zoo, go inside, and await further instructions."

Lock started the engine, put the car into gear, and drove towards the exit. Next to him, Ty still looked puzzled. "What are they thinking leaving him at a zoo?"

"They haven't. This is just part of the dance," said Lock.

"What dance?" Yuksia asked him.

"You'll see," said Lock.

13

The door opened and the guard walked in. Michael tensed a little as the he walked behind him. A second later he felt a black fabric hood being pulled down over his head. A mouth slit allowed him to breathe, but he couldn't see anything.

There was a click as the hand and foot restraints he'd been wearing since the incident with the razor blade were unlocked. Michael reached back and felt the outline of the razor blade in his back pocket. He had taken it out of the razor again after he had finished shaving, while the guard had been distracted by a phone call. But before he could use it, more guards had appeared and shackled him.

He moved his hand away as an arm wedged itself under his armpit and he was helped to his feet. He was slowly guided forward towards the door and out into the corridor.

He could hear another man talking to the guard. They were speaking Hungarian. Michael had picked up a few words, but not enough to follow the conversation. The second man took his other arm, and said in English, "Be careful. There are stairs."

With one of them on either side they walked him down a flight of stairs. He stumbled a few times and they had to tighten their grip to prevent him from falling.

He felt a breeze. He could smell petrol. After weeks alone in the room every new smell and sensation prickled his senses. He felt like a man who had been in a coma. His world, which had been so narrow and confined, was simultaneously familiar and fresh. It left his nerves raw.

The wind picked up. He shivered a little with the cold. They were definitely outside. He was sure of it.

The sound of a car engine springing to life close by startled him enough to make him jump. Next to him the two men laughed at his reaction. The second man, the one whose voice he was sure he hadn't heard before but who had spoken to him in English said, "Relax, Michael. You are going home."

Michael swallowed hard. There was something about the word 'home' that set him on edge. "Not until I know Katya's safe. I want to see her. Take me to her."

The men laughed. The second man said something to the other in Hungarian. He heard Katya's name in the mix somewhere. Michael didn't understand that they'd said but it elicited another huge belly laugh from his regular guard.

Michael felt a mixture of longing and rage flare up inside him. He would make them pay. Not now perhaps, but they would.

He felt a hand push down on the top of his head as he was bundled into what he could only imagine was the back seat of a car. The two men pressed in on either side of him, making escape impossible. He heard the car's doors slam shut. Someone switched on the radio. The car began to move.

Michael sunk back into the seat. He took as deep a breath as the hood would allow, and closed his eyes.

14

The chatter of monkeys filled the air. A group of school kids snaked past the enclosure where Lock was standing hand in hand with Yuksia. Across from them, Ty did a bad job of pretending to study a map of the zoo. Behind Ty, a heavyset local in a black leather jacket that hadn't been tailored to accommodate steroid heavy biceps the size of volleyballs was doing an equally bad surveillance job.

"So why are you so sure that they haven't left him here?" Yuksia asked Lock.

Lock was aware of the man in the leather jacket's eyes on them. He leaned in and kissed Yuksia on the lips.

"Ryan!" she protested. "We're working."

He nuzzled her neck, his lips obscured by her long hair. "Keep looking at me. There's a guy over there watching us. He's here to make sure that it's just us and that we don't have the cops in tow. That's why they wanted us somewhere public and out in the open. It means they can get a good look. But this isn't a collection point."

He gave her another kiss. In a few moments Yuksia would get another call from András with the actual collection point. It was a shame. Lock could have happily spent the day kissing Yuksia at various tourist spots around Budapest.

Right on cue her cell phone rang. The heavy was already waddling off, no doubt going to see his buddies in the Great Ape House. Ty watched him go.

Yuksia finished the call. She took Lock's hand again. "You like being right, don't you?"

Lock smiled. "You don't have to hold my hand anymore. Our shadow's gone."

Yuksia looked up at him, her chin jutting out defiantly. "I don't have to do anything. But maybe I want to."

They turned and headed for the exit. Getting on the plane to London was going to be a hell of a lot tougher than Lock had ever imagined.

15

The car came to a stop. The engine noise died. No one moved. Crammed between the two men, the pressure on Michael's left side eased suddenly as one of them opened the rear passenger door and got out. Moments later the other guard opened his door and exited the vehicle.

A hand grabbed Michael's arm, he winced as fingers pinched his bicep. He was half-guided, half-hauled from the back seat. One man either side, they marched him forwards. They were walking so quickly he struggled to keep up. Not being able to see had slowed him down.

There was the sound of a door being opened. What little light he had through the fabric of the hood faded. They were inside. The echo of their footsteps told him that much.

They kept walking, the pace a little more leisurely. Michael guessed that the speed was connected to their risk of exposure. They were more likely to be spotted outside. Even the most fleeting glance of two large men frog-marching a hooded man in a suit from a car into a building would be enough to prompt a phone call to the police.

They came to a stop again. There was the creak of another door being opened. He was pushed forward. A hand on his shoulders forced him down into a seat. His hands were pulled behind the back of the chair. His wrists were pressed together. He felt rope being tied around them.

"Stay here," he was told. "Someone will come get you soon. It's over, so relax, and forget about your whore."

The last word triggered something in him. He lashed out with a kick but the man's footsteps were already receding into the distance. The door opened and then closed again.

He was alone again. He took a breath. His rage burning afresh as he tried to reach back and dig a finger into his back pocket, searching the tiny blade.

16

The sky a burnished gold, they were losing light as Lock spun the wheel, taking a sharp right turn into an old industrial area of abandoned open lots and derelict warehouses. Lock slowed down, dropped one hand from the wheel, reached into his jacket and came up with his gun. Ty had already drawn his. Both men scanned the terrain ahead.

Yuksia was on the phone to András. He was on an open line to one of the kidnappers who was giving András, what he had promised, a final set of directions to Michael Lane.

Lock could tell from Yuksia's body language that she felt uncomfortable. He didn't blame her. Not after having been fired on the previous evening. Robertson may have seen it as a warning to stay within the usual parameters, but that was an easy call when you were tucked up in a cozy conference room at a luxury hotel. Organized crime gangs in central and Eastern Europe may not have been as quick to temper or unpredictable as say an Islamist terrorist group, but they weren't exactly a bunch of choir boys either. If they wanted to dissuade future investigations into how they targeted Western businessmen then killing Lock, Ty and Yuksia would make for an effective way of doing that.

Conversation in the car had died away. They had reached a long row of gray communist-era concrete buildings. "The third one down," Yuksia said. "They're saying he's in there."

Lock's eyes flicked to Ty, then to the building that Yuksia was pointing at, and then to his rearview mirror. The area was a maze with row after row of warehouses on both sides separated by narrow alleyways. A car could pull out behind them and they'd have no way of seeing it until it was right up their tail. Worse, Lock hadn't seen another vehicle or person in the past two minutes. If they were ambushed, they would have to fight their way out. Lock was starting to regret not taking up the offer from the manager of the gun range of some more heavy duty hardware than a couple of handguns and a half dozen fifteen round clips.

He turned round in a wide sweep and stopped next to the warehouse. He left the engine running, and got out. Ty met him on his side of the car. Lock opened the rear door and put Yuksia in the driver's seat with strict instructions to get the hell out of there if she heard so much as a single shot.

"And leave you here?" she protested.

For the very first time he regretted, if only for an instant, their brief sexual encounter. Emotion had entered what was best kept as a strictly business relationship. In his business emotion tended to get people hurt. "Yes," he said, firmly. "You can't get us help if you've been shot."

Ty had moved away from the car. Lock watched as Ty walked away slowly, his back to the concrete walls. Ty disappeared around a corner only to appear again a few moments later. He waved Lock over to him. Lock took Yuksia's hand and gave it a squeeze before turning away.

"There's a door down here," Ty said to him.

Lock stopped at the corner. Yuksia was staring at him. Reluctantly, she got into the driver's seat and closed the door.

He followed Ty to the door. They took a side each. Ty pushed the handle down. The door opened. Lock pushed through, his SIG punched out ahead of him.

Inside, the space was mostly taken up by what looked like an old printing press. Lock took a few steps inside. Ty joined him. The wind caught the door, slamming it shut behind them.

Lock waved Ty to one side of the vast metal printing press as he skirted round the other side. They were headed for what the kidnappers had told András was an operating room at the back where they would find Michael Lane.

About twenty feet ahead, Lock could see a red door. There was a faded black and white plastic sign tacked to it with wording in Hungarian. The door was slightly ajar. Lock stepped to the hinge side of the door. He pushed the door open with the toe of his boot as Ty arrived on the other side.

This time Ty pushed through the door first, gun drawn, body low as Lock provided cover. The room was completely dark. Lock doubted the building still had power, but reached out to a set of three switches and flicked them on. Miraculously, they worked. Overhead a single bare bulb flickered into life.

The two men exchanged a look at what they saw. Ty muttered a low "What the hell?" His exclamation was met with a shrug. "The hell if I know," said Lock.

Lock dug his cell phone out of his pocket, and scrolled down to Robertson's number. He hit the red call button and waited for it to connect, not entirely sure how he was going to break the news. This was one scenario they hadn't prepared for.

Ty tapped Lock's shoulder and pointed to the door. Both men spun round, guns punched out as they heard someone walking towards the room. Lock's finger fell to the trigger, ready to fire.

Yuksia appeared in the doorway. Lock lowered his weapon, ready to remonstrate with her. She stared beyond both of them to the empty chair and the floor where several lengths of thin blue rope and a black hood lay on the floor.

"Hello! Hello? Ryan?"

Robertson was shouting down the phone at Lock. Lock raised the cell to his ear. "I'm here."

From outside came the revving of a car engine. Lock hit the door first, followed closely by Ty. They raced across the printing plant floor. Ty's long legs outpaced Lock and Yuksia. Yuksia was cursing at herself in Hungarian. She transitioned to English as they got outside. "The keys! I left them in the ignition!"

Lock rounded the corner to see the car swerve to avoid hitting Ty and accelerate away at speed. At the wheel was Michael Lane.

17

S tanding next to bags packed for a flight they were set to miss, Lock stood with Yuksia at the window of Robertson's hotel suite overlooking the Chain Bridge.

Her hand settled on his shoulder. "There was nothing you could do. It was my mistake."

Behind them, Robertson was hunched at his desk, midway through a tense call to the insurance broker back in the Lloyds building in London. The broker was understandably furious at having just paid out a sizable ransom without actually having a living, breathing hostage in return.

Equally tense calls had been made to Michael Lane's wife and elderly parents, as well as his anxious employers. A few feet away from Robertson, Ty was taking the opportunity to raid the negotiator's mini bar for bars of freshly replenished Toblerone.

Like a lot of former military personnel, Ty had seen enough of the rage and despair the world had to offer not to be blown off course by what he regarded as a temporary setback to their plans. Ty's analysis of what may have motivated Michael Lane to flee a safe return home had been pithily summed up earlier when he'd told Lock, "Dude's not had a beer or seen a woman in months. I'd have split too." Yuksia had rolled her eyes at Ty's pithy summation of Lane's probable motive while Lock did his best not to laugh.

Robertson put the phone down. "Ryan, you and Tyrone don't have to stick around. It's hardly your, or Yuksia's fault that our hostage decided to take off like a bat out of hell. It's not something we legislate for. You'll be paid as agreed. I settled that with the broker."

Lock turned from his position by the window. "As far as I'm concerned the job's not finished until we have Michael Lane and we know he's safe."

"You don't have to..." Robertson started.

"I know we don't," said Lock. "But we will. Otherwise next week or next month there'll be another Michael Lane."

Robertson got up from his desk and joined Lock at the window. For a few moments the two men stood in silence, staring out at the Danube and the glittering bridge.

Lock turned back towards András who was sat on one of the suite's plush couches, his head in his hands. "Can you hit up whatever contacts you have and put the word out that we're offering five thousand euro for any information leading to us finding Michael Lane?"

András grabbed his cell phone and set to work. "What about the media? We can tell them he's a missing person. Make up some story that he's had a breakdown."

"Good idea, but let's save it for tomorrow. If we can't find him by then we can go the public appeal route. Yuksia, Ty, you're with me."

Ty tossed a chocolate wrapper into a wastepaper basket. "Where we going?"

"Lane's apartment. He's going to need money, a change of clothes."

Yuksia didn't move. She had taken her screw up of leaving the keys in the car pretty hard.

"Yuksia?" said Lock.

She looked over at him. "You really want me to help you after what happened?"

"We need you," said Lock. "I need you. Now, let's save the postmortem for when this is done. We have to find this man before it's too late. So far he's not exactly made the best decisions. In his current mental state I don't see that changing."

18

Heart thumping, Michael Lane pulled into a quiet side street just off Arany János Street. He switched off the engine of the Skoda, got out, locked the car and pocketed the key fob.

He briskly walked the quarter mile to his apartment. He scanned the front entrance. Everything appeared normal.

Stomping his feet to try and force some heat into them, he waited until a neighbor was leaving, kept his head down, brushed past them before the door closed again, and walked inside. He took the stairs up to his apartment. Fingers crossed, he lifted the door mat outside the front door. The key he had left for Katya was still there, undisturbed since he had left to go to work all those weeks ago.

Slowly, he turned the key in the lock, and opened the door. Inside, the apartment was empty. But someone had been here. He could tell from the open drawers in one of the bedrooms.

He only stayed long enough to grab some cash, a credit card, and fresh clothes. He exited the building less than five minutes later wearing a raincoat and with a wool cap pulled down low over his eyes. Tucked inside his coat was one other item – a large Sabatier knife plucked from the butcher's block that sat on the kitchen counter next to the range.

Outside, he walked the few short steps to József Attila Street, flagged down a yellow taxi, and gave the driver the address. He settled back into the seat and closed his eyes.

THE TAXI CAB pulled up a few doors short of the club on Rózsa Street in District 6. The entrance was guarded by two imposing doormen. For a second, Michael almost lost his nerve. He paid the driver, took a deep breath and stopped out of the cab. Keeping his head down, he walked straight past the two doormen and inside the club.

It took a moment for his eyes to adjust to the gloom. Scantily clad young women moved among the mostly British and German tourists hustling for business. Michael stood near a railing at the back of the club and scanned the stage where a young blond woman was busy gyrating around a pole while a stag party of drunken Brits screamed various obscenities at her. One of the men in the party jammed a hand down his pants and started to masturbate, cheered on by his pals. The girl on stage, her eyes glazed over, kept dancing as the DJ turned up the music to drown out the catcalls.

Michael kept scanning the crowd. It had been a long shot. There was very little chance that Katya would be back working here. Not after her promise to him.

Finally, in a booth off to one corner, Michael spotted a girl he recognized. She was gyrating her hips against the groin of a disheveled middle-aged businessman. The girl grabbed his tie and pulled the man's face down towards her bare breasts. The man grinned idiotically and reached back to grab her ass only to have his hand slapped away.

Michael pushed his way through the crush towards the girl. She looked up from her lap dance as he approached. She leaned in and kissed the businessman on the cheek, her lipstick leaving a perfect kiss-shaped smear that marked him out as hers. She patted his knee and walked over to meet Michael.

"I'm looking for Katya," he shouted over the din.

The dancer motioned for him to follow him. There were private areas in the back of the club where the dancers could negotiate with client for extra services not suited to public performance. Michael hesitated but trotted after her as she turned and walked through a bead curtain.

The swell of the music fell away. She turned to face him. The wide smile she maintained for the customers fell away, replaced by a look that fell halfway between a sneer and a snarl. "You want to find Katya?" she said to him.

He dug into his pocket and came up with a bundle of notes. He knew what motivated the dancers. "Here, if you can tell me where she is you can keep it all. There's more too. I need to find her."

She laughed, reached out and took the notes. "You really want to know where she is?"

Michael glanced around. If one of the club's security had seen him coming back here then he was in big trouble. "That's what I just said. Now can you help me?"

The dancers hand's fell to her hips. She looked him up and down. "You are a stupid man. She is with Hugo. You know, her husband. Michael, she was always with Hugo."

The impact of what she was saying sent Michael stumbling back. His face flushed. He felt like he might be able to vomit. "What are you talking about?"

"What did she tell you? That she loved you? It's the game. You think you just happened to run into her that evening in the park? That was it a coincidence like in some dumb American romance movie. It was all planned. Now you had better get out of here. And if you tell anyone what I told you then I'll make you regret it, Michael."

She strode past him, brushed through the curtain, and disappeared, leaving behind the smell of sweat, stale cigarette smoke, and perfume. Michael struggled to process what she had just said. How did she know where he had met Katya? It couldn't have been a set-up. Hugo must have paid her to tell him this story so that he would give up looking for Katya. Katya wasn't married. And not to Hugo. He was her boss. That was all. Katya had been married. But her husband had died, hit by a train outside St Petersburg, leaving her, at the age of just seventeen, as a widow with a small child to look after and no parents to help. That was how she had fallen into this life.

In a daze, Michael walked back into the club. The two doormen were at the bar, scanning the crowd. Michael knew who they were looking for. He turned round and headed back the way he'd come.

One of the bouncers spotted him. He nudged the other one. They began to shove their way through the crowd, elbowing people out of the way. A drunken tourist took a swing at one of them, and was quickly felled by a crushing elbow to his face.

Michael walked past the private booths, past a locked store room and found a fire door. He pushed through and out into a dark alley-way. He took to his heels, winded after the first fifty meters.

He stopped, doubled over, his hands on his knees as he fought catch his breath. Glancing back he saw the two super-sized doormen run into the alleyway, and look around. Michael straightened up and took off again, ignoring the searing pain in his chest, and the slowly dawning knowledge that he'd been a fool, not once, but twice, and that it might still cost him his life.

19

Ty strode into the living room of Michael Lane's apartment and began looking around. "Bedroom's clear," he announced.

Lock had turned on the iMac and was checking the history on the Safari browser. It made for interesting reading, but the last time it had been used was the evening before the abduction. The last few websites Michael had been looking at related to international sex trafficking. He had also looked up the British visa requirements for a Russian national looking to relocate to the United Kingdom on a permanent basis.

The toilet flushed and a few moments later Yuksia emerged from the bathroom. She glanced over Lock's shoulder at the computer screen. "Anything?"

Lock shook his head. He closed the browser window, and got up from the desk. He followed Yuksia through into the kitchen. She opened one of the cabinets, took out a package of coffee, opened it and smelled to see if it was fresh.

Something caught Lock's eye. *The presence of the abnormal. The absence of the normal.* He stepped around Yuksia who was busy starting to make coffee.

The wooden knife block sitting next to the cooking range had an empty slot. Going by the arrangement of the knives, and the position and size of the slot, the knife that was missing was one of the larger blades.

Lock pulled one of the remaining knives from the block as Ty came in. Lock held up the knife. "Check the drawers. See if you can find a bigger one of these knives."

Yuksia helped them look. They rifled drawer and cupboard. No knife. The set remained incomplete.

"Ty, check the bedroom again. If he felt like he was under threat before the abduction, he might have kept it handy," said Lock.

Lock walked into the hallway. It wasn't there. A few minutes passed. Ty returned. "Maybe it broke. Or a neighbor borrowed it," said Ty.

"No. It was here before. I'm sure of it," Lock said. "He's been back here."

"So where is he now?" Yuksia asked.

20

Both András and Robertson jumped up from their seats as the designated kidnap phone began to ring. The two men traded a look. Robertson picked up one of the pair of headphones plugged into the handset, while András grabbed the headset with the microphone. Robertson reached over and activated the recorder. It was only then that he gave András the thumbs up. They were running silent.

"This is András," he said in Hungarian.

András didn't recognize the voice of the man on the other end of the line. He sounded older and more cultured than the person he had had been dealing with before. His accent was more Russian than Hungarian, the tone more polished.

"Put your boss on the line," the man said in English.

András glanced over at Robertson. Robertson motioned for András to hand him his headset. The two men swapped.

"This is Robertson. Who am I speaking to?"

For a second Robertson thought The Russian may have hung up. His question was met by silence. Robertson didn't say anything. The Russian was either still there or he wasn't. By prompting him, Robertson would be conceding ground, and indicating his own anxiety. Silence was one of the most powerful weapons in a negotiation between two parties.

"I gave you back Michael Lane. I held up my end of the bargain. But now he is causing trouble for me." The Russian paused. "I'm sorry. This is out of my control now."

Robertson started to speak, but The Russian was gone. Robertson slammed his hand down hard onto the table. He wrenched off the headset and threw it down. He walked to the window, grabbed his cell phone from his pants pocket, and scrolled down until he reached Lock's number. It didn't take a genius to work out what The Russian had just told him.

21

The streets were quiet, save for the distant sound of late night revelers heading home. Michael Lane kept walking, checking over his shoulder every few feet to make sure he wasn't being followed.

He turned a corner onto Andrassy Avenue, Budapest's main shopping street. A dark-colored 5-Series BMW was parked facing him, its engine idling. Its lights blazed suddenly to life. His heart skipped a couple of beats.

The BMW pulled out into traffic. He caught sight of a middle-aged woman at the wheel. He relaxed a notch, but he couldn't stay out here. They'd find him. It was only a matter of time.

He had to get to the airport. They surely wouldn't try to take him from a busy airport terminal with all its security. If he could just get a flight to London then he'd be safe. But first he had to make one last trip back to his apartment to pick up the passport he'd stupidly forgotten to collect on his last brief visit.

He had the plan in his mind. In and out. Grab the passport. Take a taxi to the airport. Get on the last flight to London, or the first one leaving the next morning if he had already missed the evening flight. He could sleep in the terminal if he had to.

22

L ock glanced at his watch. It was twenty-three minutes after midnight. The last flight to London had long since departed. *So much for easy money. So much for forty-eight hours in Budapest.*

Lock listened carefully to what Robertson was telling him. He thanked him for the information, and ended the call. Ty and Yuksia looked at him.

"It's real simple," said Lock. "We have to find Michael Lane before they do."

"And if we don't?" said Ty.

"Then he's still going home. Only he'll be in a wooden box in the hold."

23

The white builder's truck turned the corner onto Hild tér. An elderly man walking a small herd of terriers hurried them along as they snapped in the direction of the truck. The truck came to a stop. Two men got out of the front cab. They moved to the back of the truck, and opened the rear doors. One man climbed up into the back of the truck and pushed a thick roll of plastic sheeting over the lip of the truck bed. The other man grabbed the end and they slowly hauled the roll of sheeting up the steps to the apartment entrance.

A third man stepped from the lobby's shadows, and unlocked the door. He held the door open for the two men. They moved inside. He closed the door behind them. They edged up two more steps, and took a left, making for the main stairway. It split in two directions. They went left.

With much grunting and heaving, the two men carried the roll of sheeting up the stairs. As they reached the first landing, they paused to catch their breath. The third man moved ahead of them. Once they had caught their breath, they began to climb the next set of stairs.

In under ten minutes, they had reached the third floor landing. The man who had been waiting for them in the lobby took out a key.

He opened the door into Michael Lane's apartment. He held the door open for the two men. They moved past him. Once they had moved clear of the door, he closed it.

They dumped the roll on the floor. The third man killed the lights, plunging the living room into darkness save for the street lights outside on József Attila Street. One of the men dug out a pack of cigarettes. He tapped out a cigarette from the pack and produced a small plastic lighter. As he flicked a thumb at the wheel, the third man snatched the lighter from his hand. Cigarette smoke would be a giveaway that someone was in the apartment

"You can smoke when we're finished," he said, stepping into the kitchen, opening a drawer and pulling out a heavy pair of scissors.

"Which room?" asked the first of the moving men.

The supervisor nodded behind them towards the spare bedroom. He took out a piece of paper with the room's dimensions, including the ceiling height from his jacket pocket. He laid it out flat on the breakfast bar. Using the torch light on his cell phone, he showed them the measurements. They would need to cut six pieces of the heavy black plastic sheeting – one for each wall, and one each for the ceiling and floor.

Dismemberment could be a messy business. The third man had argued with Hugo about the location. It involved unnecessary risk. It would be easier to take the Englishman back to the printing plant, or to another location entirely. But The Russian had been adamant. He wanted to send a signal.

To kill a man in some unseen location was shocking. To cut him into pieces inside his own home – a home that lay in the heart of the city's most upmarket district – would send a much stronger signal. The Russian and his wife already had three new prospects lined up. One was the CEO of a German bank. The Russian saw this as the best way of making sure that he would not be messed around in future.

The third man nodded to the others. "Come on. We have a room to re-decorate."

24

Michael Lane stood directly outside the apartment door and took a deep breath. Beyond the frosted glass and metal grille of the door, the apartment lay in darkness. As quietly as he could, he turned the key in the lock, and slowly pushed the door open. He pulled the key back out, and jammed it back into his pocket. He pulled the knife from inside his coat, and gripped the handle.

The blade still in his hand, he stepped into the open plan kitchen/living area. Apart from the green tinged dots of light from the digital displays of the oven and microwave, it was pitch black. He looked across at the glass doors in the living room that led out to the balcony.

The metal storm shutters were down. He was sure they had been up when he'd left. He tightened his grip on the handle of the knife.

He took another step forward. As he put his foot down, a hand came from nowhere and clamped across his mouth. Another hand gripped his wrist, levering it painfully back. Pain shot up his arm. His grip loosened. The Sabatier knife fell from his grasp and clattered onto the wooden floor.

The lights came on. The person holding him leaned in to whisper in his ear as Michael got sight of three men sitting like a row of ducks on the couch in the living room. Their hands and feet were tied with various items of his clothing. Socks had been jammed into their mouths to keep them from talking. He was sure he recognized at least one of the men from the night club.

Facing the three men was a tall, white man with short hair. He had a handgun pointed at the three bound men. He glanced across at Michael with a smile. He looked completely in control and perfectly relaxed, as if holding three men at gunpoint was an everyday occurrence.

The man with the gun spoke. "We're here to take you home to London, Michael. But we're going to need you to do exactly what we say, when we say it. If you don't then we might as well just let Grumpy, Dopey, and Happy here finish turning that room back there into a wet room, and slice you up for dog food."

The three men on the couch glared at the man standing over them as he continued talking. "That's what you were doing, right? Little bit of late night remodeling." He turned back to Michael. "Now, can Tyrone here let go of you without any further incident?"

The iron grip around Michael's mouth, loosened just enough that he could nod his head. The massive scoop of a hand fell away. Slowly he half-turned to see the man who had grabbed him. He was bigger than the man with the gun, a tall, dark sheet of muscle that towered over everyone else in the room. He exuded a controlled menace. It came off him in waves. The three thugs sitting quietly on the couch suddenly made sense.

There was the sound of footsteps. A young Hungarian women with dark hair walked through from the master bedroom. She ignored Michael and addressed the man with the gun. "Ryan, a car just pulled up outside with four men inside."

25

A s Yuksia watched, Lock flicked a coin in the air, caught it, and slapped his right hand down on top of it. He looked at Ty. "Heads or tails?"

Ty called heads. Lock pulled his hand away to reveal that it was tails.

"Best out of three?" he said to Ty.

"No," said Ty. "Don't have time for that bullshit. I got this."

The decision made, Lock grabbed Michael's elbow and guided him back towards to the apartment door. Yuksia followed close behind. At the door, Lock glanced back towards Ty.

"You sure?" Lock said to his partner.

Ty squared his broad shoulders and glanced towards the balcony. "Get the hell out of here."

The last thing Lock, Yuksia, and Michael heard as they stepped out into the dimly lit corridor was the sound of Ty racking back the slide of his SIG Sauer 229.

Michael looked back anxiously at the apartment. "I'm sorry for putting you guys in this position," he said to Lock.

Lock pulled his weapon, and made sure he stayed in front of

Michael as they started to climb the stairs. "You want to make it up to us? Do exactly what I tell to you do, when I tell you."

"Of course," said Michael.

As SOON AS they were gone, Ty walked across the living room, and hit the switch to raise the electrically powered shutters. The smaller of the three men was moving his head from side to side, and trying to speak. Ty crossed to him and pulled the sock from his mouth.

The man stared at him. "Our friends will be here soon. When they get here we will take you into the room back there. You have not experienced pain like we will make for you," He rocked his head back in the direction of the spare bedroom.

Ty loomed over him. He opened his left hand and tapped the man's face with his open palm, just hard enough to get his attention. "Whatever you say, Chief. As for pain, you ain't met some of my ex-girlfriends. You ever date a girl from Long Beach called Kwaneesha? Now *that's* pain."

Ty grabbed the sock and jammed it back into the man's mouth. He grabbed the back of the man's collar, and pulled him up from the couch. With his hands tied behind his back, the man's own weight took him forward, and he fell face first onto the floor. There was a crunch of bone as his nose made contact with the walnut hardwood floor. The man let out a muffled cry of pain. Ty jammed the heel of his boot down into the small of the man's back for a brief moment.

The other two men were looking at Ty. He turned towards them, the barrel of the SIG pointed at them. "Anyone else have anything they want to share with me?" Ty asked them.

They shook their heads frantically back and forth.

"Yeah, that's what I figured," said Ty.

Ty opened the door that led out onto the small stone balcony as a fire alarm out in the corridor began to wail. Next, he walked back into the master bedroom, and began stripping the sheets from the bed. He took out his Gerber and began cutting the sheets lengthways into strips. When he was done cutting, he began to braid the strips together.

THE BROKEN GLASS from the fire alarm on the top floor corridor lay at Lock's feet. He crossed to the three apartment doors and began to bang on them with his fist. Lights flickered on, and people began to shout behind the frosted glass doors. Before anyone could come out, Lock pointed towards a door on the other side of the corridor. "That go to the roof?" he asked Michael.

"Yes, I've been up there with..." said Michael, breaking off. "Yes, it takes you onto the roof."

"And there's one of the other side of the building?" Lock asked him.

"Yes," Michael said.

"Perfect," said Lock, taking a step back and aiming a kick at the door.

The door flew open. Lock grabbed hold off Michael and they pushed through. Directly ahead of them was a ladder leading upwards into darkness. "You go first," Lock told Yuksia.

Yuksia grabbed for the ladder and started to climb. Michael went next. Lock went last.

It was a short climb. Fifteen rungs. They reached the top. There was another door. It was unlocked. They were on the roof. Michael and Yuksia followed Lock as he walked across the roof to a matching door. Beyond the door was a ladder leading down to the top floor of the building's other side. Because the building was split, and perfectly symmetrical, they could walk down the stairs on the other side without any risk of running into the men who were heading for Michael's apartment. Of course, that was assuming they hadn't split up. If they had, thought Lock, he had fifteen rounds in his clip, more than enough to take care of the situation if he absolutely had to.

TY LEANED over the edge of the balcony and looked down to the street

below. He could see the car that Yuksia had warned them about. The
driver was smoking a cigarette with the window down. He had a skin-
head haircut and was squeezed into a dark suit that looked like it had
been tailored for a man ten pounds lighter. That meant, if Yuksia's
count was correct, that there were three men on the way up to the
apartment to check on their compatriots.

Right on cue there was a banging on the door and a man shouting
urgently in what Ty assumed was Hungarian. Ty pulled out his cell
phone and hit Lock's name. It took a moment to connect. "I got them
here. You should be clear."

Marching back into the living room, Ty walked across to the man
lying face down on the floor, blood still pouring from his nose, and
hauled him up onto his knees. "Okay, I know you speak English, so
I'm going to take the gag out, and you're going to tell your buddies
outside that everything's cool and that they're not needed. You cross
me and you're going to be minus one of your knee caps. You
feel me?"

The man nodded.

LOCK HOLSTERED his gun as they headed back down the stairs on the
opposite side of the building. On every floor, residents were
appearing from their apartments in pajamas and dressing gowns,
reluctantly making their down to the front entrance. Lock, Yuksia,
and Michael fell in with them. One or two people shot them a suspicious look, but no one said anything.

They reached the ground floor, and headed, along with everyone
else, for the lobby. A fire truck had just pulled up outside.

"Keep your heads down, and keep walking," Lock instructed.

TY YANKED the sock from the man's mouth. He tapped the barrel of
the SIG against the man's temple.

"Okay, tell them it's cool," Ty whispered.

The man immediately started screaming in Hungarian. Whatever he was saying, Ty was certain that it didn't translate to, "Everything's cool."

Ty pushed the man's head back down. He pressed the barrel of the SIG into the back of the man's left knee and pulled the trigger. The man let out a high-pitched scream.

The near wall shook as one of the men standing outside threw themselves at the door. The frame shuddered, but the door held. The two men on the couch began to bounce around, no doubt aware that when their buddies made it through the door, they would likely be caught in the crossfire. Ty turned and ran for the balcony, where he had already tied off the braided sheets to a balustrade.

Holstering his SIG, he swung a long leg over the edge of the balcony, and hauled himself over the lip of the railing. He grabbed the sheet with both hands and began to move down, hand over hand. He could feel the fabric strain as soon as he let go of the concrete lip. His stomach churned with the sickening realization that it could tear at any minute.

WITH ONE HAND on Yuksia's arm, Lock pushed Michael ahead as they ran out onto Joszef Atilla Street. A black Mercedes Benz screeched to a stop next to the bus shelter. Lock opened the rear passenger door and shoved Michael into the back seat head first. He held it open for Yuksia. She hurried in. He closed the rear passenger door, and stepped back from the car.

András gunned the engine and the Benz took off, racing the short distance towards the Danube and the Chain Bridge. The bridge would take them out of Pest and into the winding streets of Buda, where Robertson was waiting for them.

On the sidewalk, Lock turned back to where he could see Ty dangling from the improvised sheet-rope about thirty feet above the street. A man appeared on the balcony of Michael Lane's apartment. In his hand was a knife. He looked around. He saw where Ty had tied off the braided sheet rope. He started towards it.

Without waiting, Lock drew his SIG, punched it out ahead of him with both hands, falling into a modified Weaver stance, and squeezed the trigger. The shot went high, pinging off the corner of the balcony above. The man ducked back inside.

Lock kept scanning the building as Ty picked up the pace, shimmying down the rope as fast as he could. The man with the knife appeared again, hunkered down low. Lock snapped into a shooting stance once more, ready to give the guy the good news if he made another move to cut the rope.

Finally, with a few feet between the soles of his boots and the sidewalk, Ty let go. He dropped down onto the sidewalk. Lock took that as his cue to move back into the shadows as Ty hugged the wall, making sure that he didn't give anyone on the balcony the angle for a shot.

Lock ran across the street and joined Ty at the corner. "You okay?" Lock asked him.

Ty glanced back in the direction of the apartment. "We should go back up there. Teach those assholes a lesson."

"Another time maybe," said Lock, as two Rendőrség police cars sped past, sirens blaring. "Right now, we need to get out of here."

The two men took off running. Three blocks later they slowed to walk. Even though they had only traveled a short distance, the streets were quiet. The old, ornate stone buildings seemed to have swallowed the chaos behind them.

They reached the Chain Bridge. Lock noted the lions on their plinths, on guard for any signs of trouble. He glanced over at Ty as they passed the midway point across the bridge. Ty's face was set.

"What's up?" Lock asked him.

Ty cleared his throat. "Next time you want to want to go away for the weekend somewhere romantic, do me a favor?"

"Sure," said Lock.

"Ask someone else," said Ty.

26

The drive to Budapest's Ferenc Liszt airport passed in tense silence. Michael Lane sat in back, sandwiched between Ty and Robertson. Lock was up front in the passenger seat, while Yuksia drove. Traffic was heavy as they moved through the run-down industrial area near the airport. Lock continually checked the cars around them for signs of Hugo or his men.

Michael had already shared with them the whole story of how he came to meet a beautiful young Russian woman while out walking. It was a chance encounter. At least that's what he had thought.

The relationship between Michael and Katya had developed quickly. He had fallen head over heels in love with her. He thought she had done the same. His marriage had already hit a rocky patch. His wife hadn't wanted him to take the job in Budapest in the first place. Michael had thought the distance might do them good. He had been wrong about that as well. His wife had refused to visit, and after he had begun to see Katya his regular trips home had become infrequent.

It was only now, with the benefit of knowing he'd been set up, that he understood that what he saw as Katya's interest in every aspect of his life, including his work, was her weighing him up as a mark. The final conversation with her had revolved around some of the rumored kidnappings that had been taking place in the city. He had revealed to Katya that he wasn't worried. If he was abducted, his company had insurance in place that covered all their employees worldwide. It had been a tiny clause in his employee package that had stuck in his mind because it seemed so outlandish.

That revelation had no doubt sealed his fate. Two days later he was being bundled at gunpoint into the car outside his apartment.

YUKSIA PULLED up outside Terminal 2B. They got out, Lock and Ty scanning the people huddled outside in the cold who had either just been dropped off or who were grabbing a final cigarette before their flight. Robertson unloaded their bags. He would be taking a later flight.

Lock went over to say goodbye to Yuksia. "You'll be safe?" he asked her.

She shrugged. "Of course."

"Maybe you can come visit me in the States?" he said.

Yuksia looked up at him, her chin jutting out. Her eyes glistened in the mineral-gray air. She stood on tip toes, put her arms around his neck, and kissed him. "It was good to meet you, Mr.. Lock. Don't spoil it now."

She was right. They both knew that this was it. It had been a moment in time. They had lives to go back to. She broke away. He reached down and took her hand. Behind Yuksia, he could see Ty growing impatient, eager to get inside the relative safety of the terminal, get checked in, and through security.

Lock squeezed Yuksia's hand. "Take care."

He let go, and turned away as Yuksia and Robertson climbed back into the black Benz. Lock watched it pull away from the curb. He followed Ty and Michael inside, and they joined the queue of passengers checking in for the London flight.

THE END

Made in United States
North Haven, CT
27 August 2022

23345799R00046